LET'S EAT!
¡A COMER!

by Pat Mora

Illustrated by Maribel Suárez

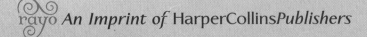
rayo *An Imprint of* HarperCollins*Publishers*

"Who's hungry?" asks Mom.

—¿Quién tiene hambre? —pregunta Mamá.

Tico starts barking. Tico is *always* hungry.

Tico empieza a ladrar, pues él *siempre* tiene hambre.

Dad and Grandma come to the table.

Papá y Abuelita vienen a la mesa.

My little sister, Tina, and my brother, Danny, come too.

Mis hermanitos, Tina y Danny, vienen también.

Tico sits and looks up at me.

Tico se sienta y me mira.

On the table, we see a big pot of beans.
Sobre la mesa vemos una olla llena de frijoles.

We see grated cheese and a bowl of chile.
Vemos el queso rallado y un cuenco de chile.

We see a stack of warm tortillas.
Vemos un montón de tortillas calientitas.

We see a green salad.
Vemos una ensalada de lechuga.

Tina says, "Look at all the food! We're rich, aren't we, Dad?"

—¡Cuánta comida! —dice Tina—. Somos ricos, ¿verdad, Papá?

Dad looks at all the good food.
Papá mira toda esa rica comida.

He looks at Mom and Grandma.
Luego mira a Mamá y a Abuelita.

He looks at Danny and Tina and me.
Nos mira a Danny, a Tina y a mí.

Tico barks, so Dad looks at Tico too.
Tico ladra, y Papá también lo mira.

"Yes," says Dad. "We're rich."

—Sí —dice Papá—. Somos muy ricos.

To Becky Brumley,
who encouraged me to write these books,
and to Oralia Garza de Cortés, literary advocate
A Becky Brumley,
quien me animó a escribir estos libros,
y a Oralia Garza de Cortés, defensora de la alfabetización
—P.M.

To my little ones—Bimba, Pavis, and Tebis
Para mis pequeños: Bimba, Pavis y Tebis
—M.S.

Rayo is an imprint of HarperCollins Publishers.

Let's Eat! / ¡A comer!
Text copyright © 2008 by Pat Mora
Illustrations copyright © 2008 by Maribel Suárez
Manufactured in China.

Library of Congress Cataloging-in-Publication Data is available.
ISBN-10: 0-06-085038-8 (trade bdg.) — ISBN-13: 978-0-06-085038-8 (trade bdg.)
ISBN-10: 0-06-085039-6 (lib. bdg.) — ISBN-13: 978-0-06-085039-5 (lib. bdg.)

Design by Stephanie Bart-Horvath
2 3 4 5 6 7 8 9 10
❖
First Edition